Text and illustrations © 1993 by Klaus Baumgart
All rights reserved. Printed in the United States of America.
© 1991 by Breitschopf Wien-Stuttgart.
First published 1991 by hpt-Verlagsgesellschaft mbH. & Co. KG, Vienna.
First published in the United States by Hyperion Books for Children,
114 Fifth Avenue, New York, New York 10011.
FIRST EDITION
1   3   5   7   9   10   8   6   4   2

Library of Congress Cataloging-in-Publication Data

Baumgart, Klaus. [Ertappt. English] Where are you, Little Green Dragon? /
Klaus Baumgart—1st ed.   p.   cm.
Summary: Anna's Little Green Dragon has
a new adventure inside the refrigerator.
ISBN 1-56282-344-2 (trade)—ISBN 1-56282-345-0 (lib. bdg.)
[1. Dragons—Fiction.   2. Refrigerators—Fiction.]   I. Title.
PZ7.B3285Wh   1993   [E]—dc20   92-72026   CIP   AC

Reprinted by arrangement with Hyperion Books for Children.

Where Are You, Little Green Dragon?

Klaus Baumgart

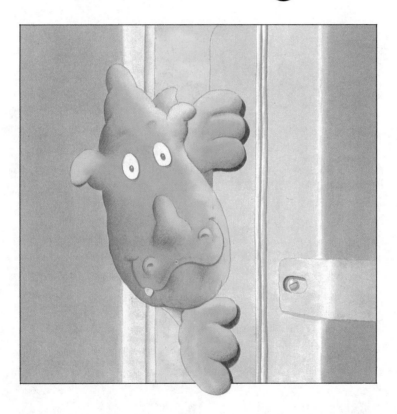

Hyperion Books for Children
New York

The Little Green Dragon is off on another wild adventure.

"Wheeeeeeee!"

He swings himself merrily through the air.

Curiously, he searches his surroundings.

Staring at him hungrily is a giant monster.
The Little Green Dragon runs for his life!

"Whew," he puffs once he is safe.
He climbs up…

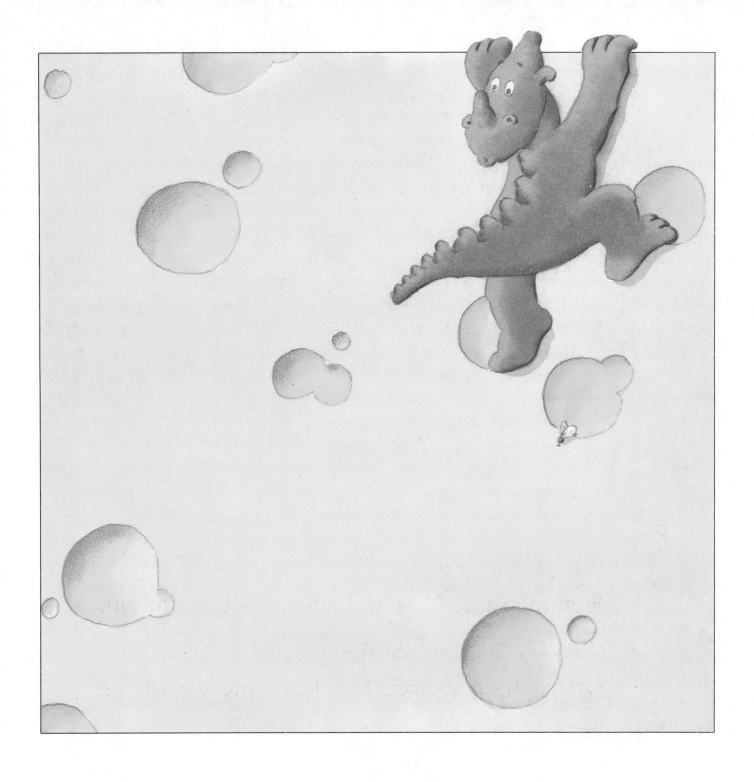

...and up.

When the Little Green Dragon reaches the top, he begins to tremble with cold.

I wish I had my scarf to keep me warm, he thinks.

But slipping and sliding on the ice is so much fun, the Little Green Dragon forgets all about the chilly air.

After a while he is ready for more adventure, so the Little Green Dragon begins the long climb down.

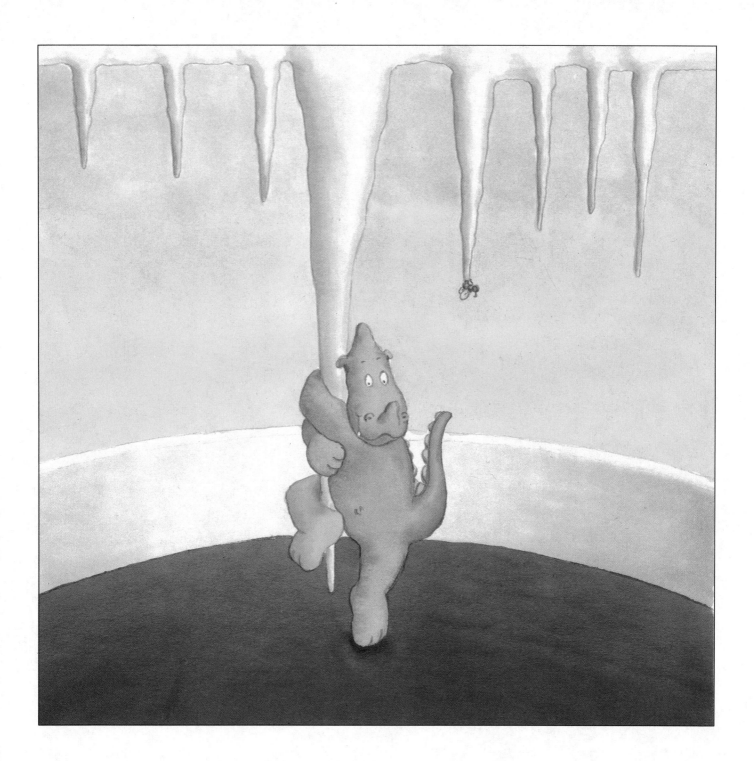

At the bottom, something feels squishy and soft and…

...it tastes quite delicious!

Just as the Little Green Dragon settles in to enjoy his snack, the refrigerator door opens.

"What are you doing in that chocolate pudding!" his friend Anna scolds.

But Anna isn't *really* mad—she just wants the
Little Green Dragon to share!